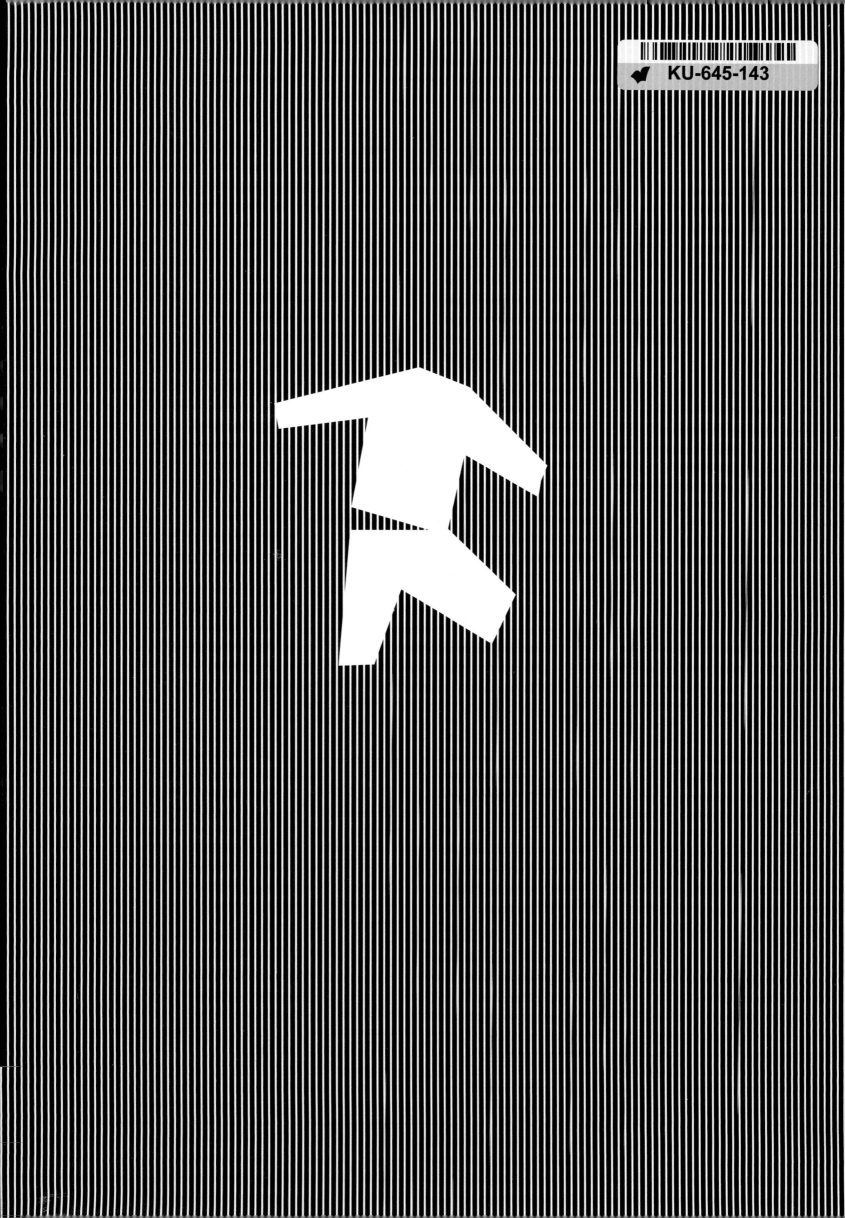

TA DA!

When my pyjamas start to whirl,
through the air I can twirl.

When the stripes start to spin,

let the adventure begin!

Will you follow me?

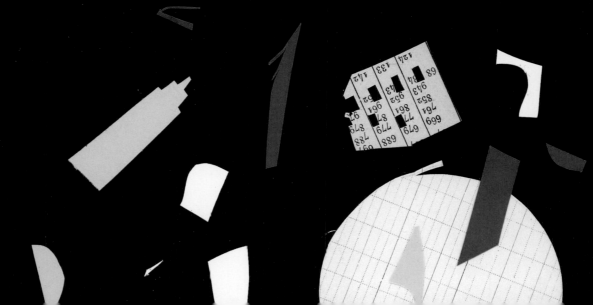

But where are we going?

The traffic whizzes in a tangled race,
But all roads lead to much the same place..

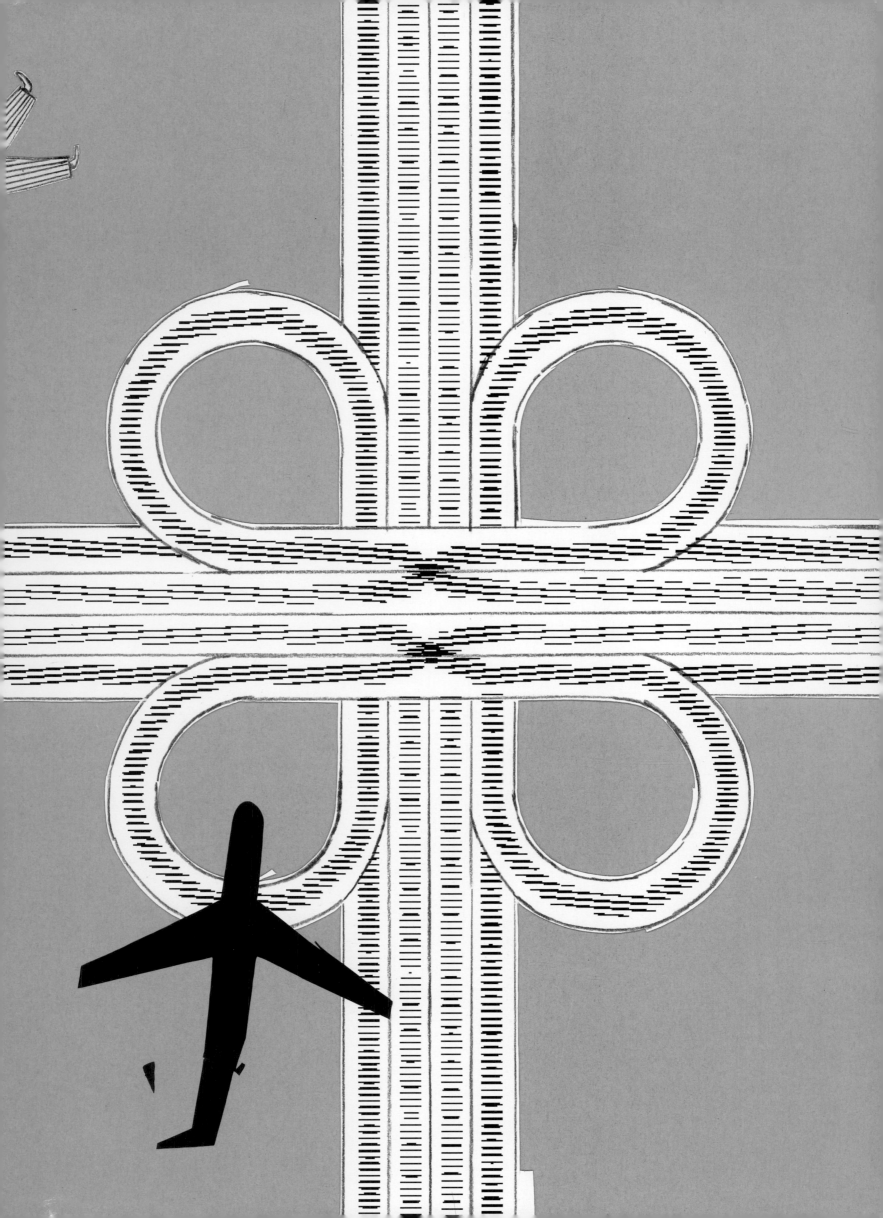

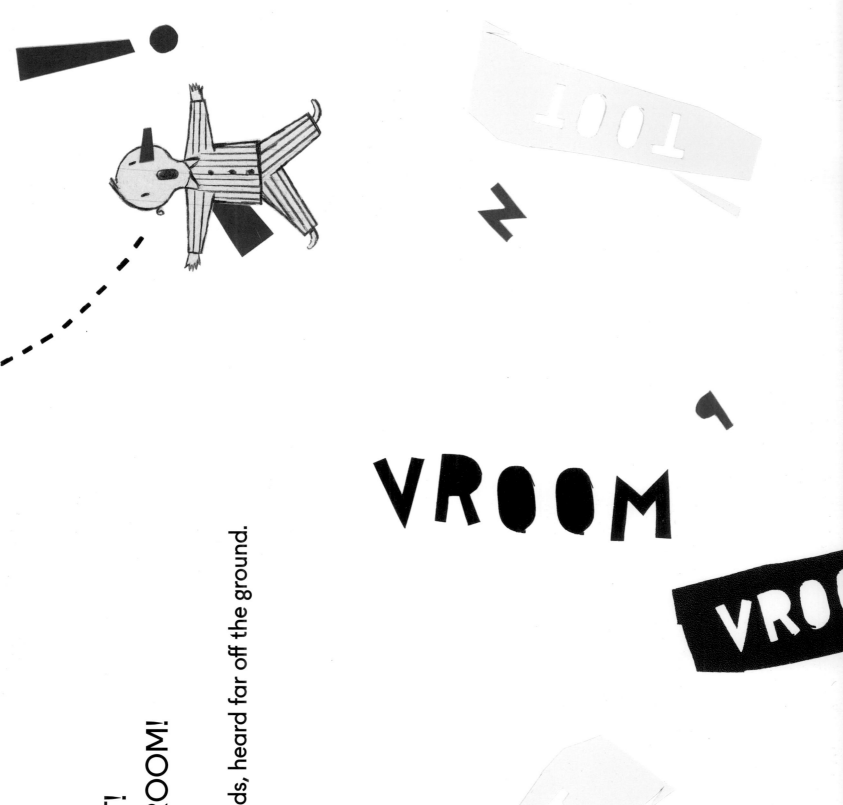

TOOT TOOT!
VROOM! VROOM!

A jungle of sounds, heard far off the ground.

SHOPPING!

WOW!
Where to look first? I can't decide.
Everything's so bright, so fast,
so tall and so wide.

And hustling and bustling,
the strangest sight ever,
Are the swarms of people
all moving together.

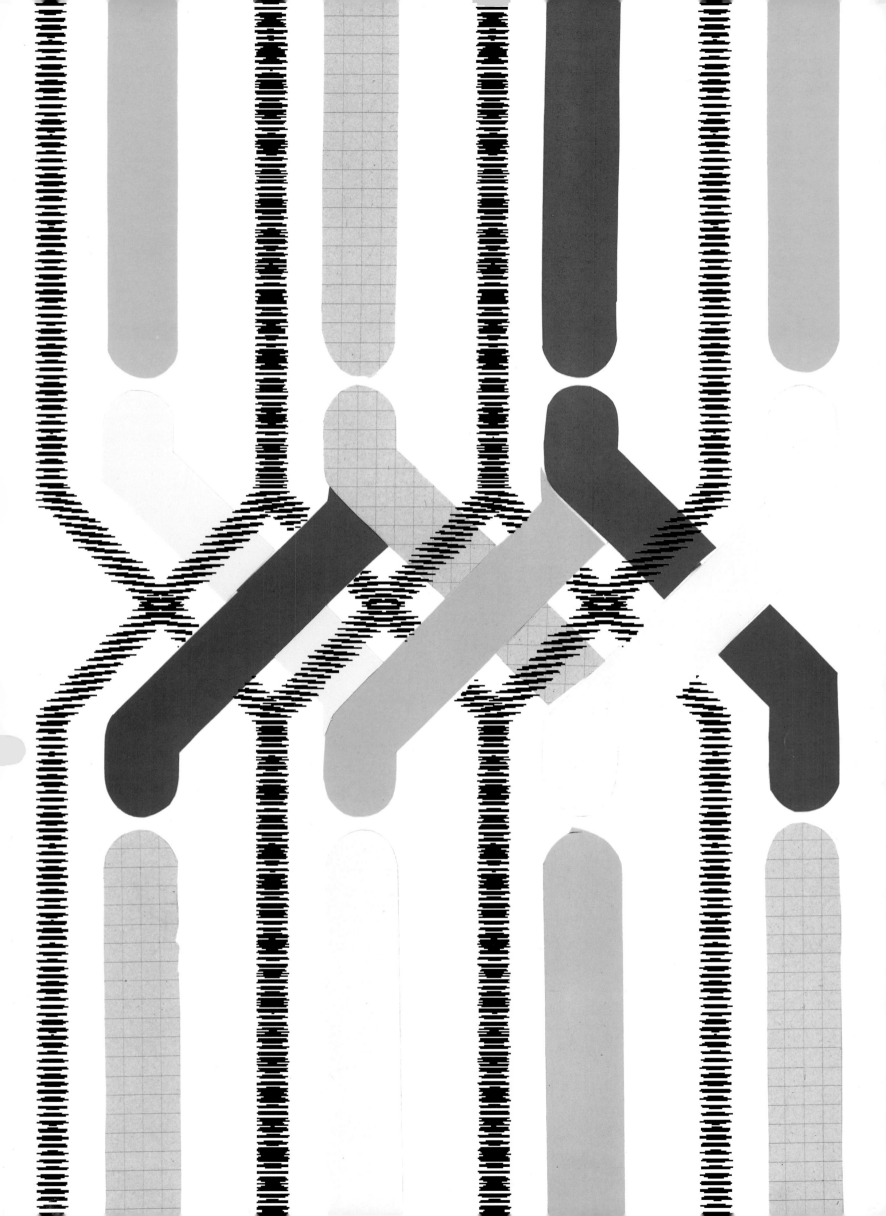

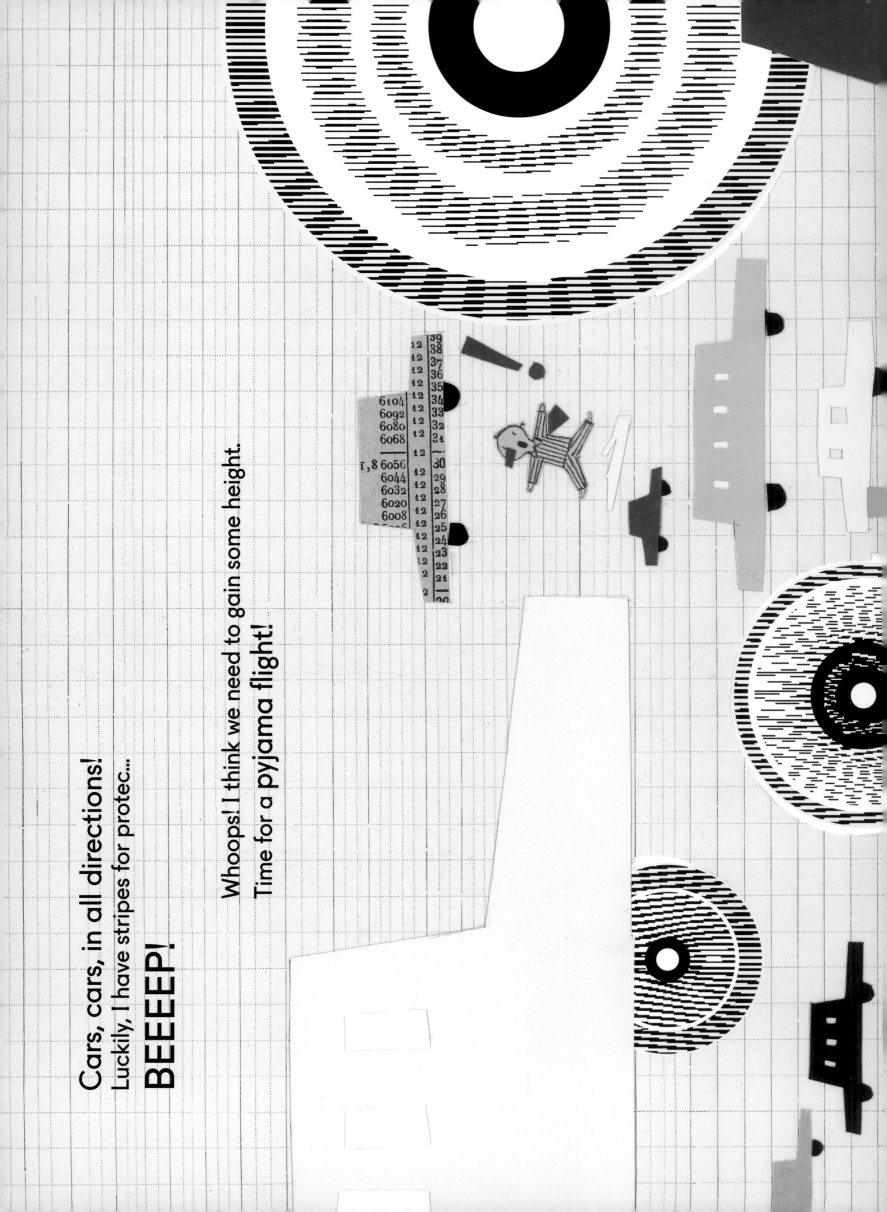

Cars, cars, in all directions!
Luckily, I have stripes for protec...
BEEEEP!

Whoops! I think we need to gain some height.
Time for a pyjama flight!

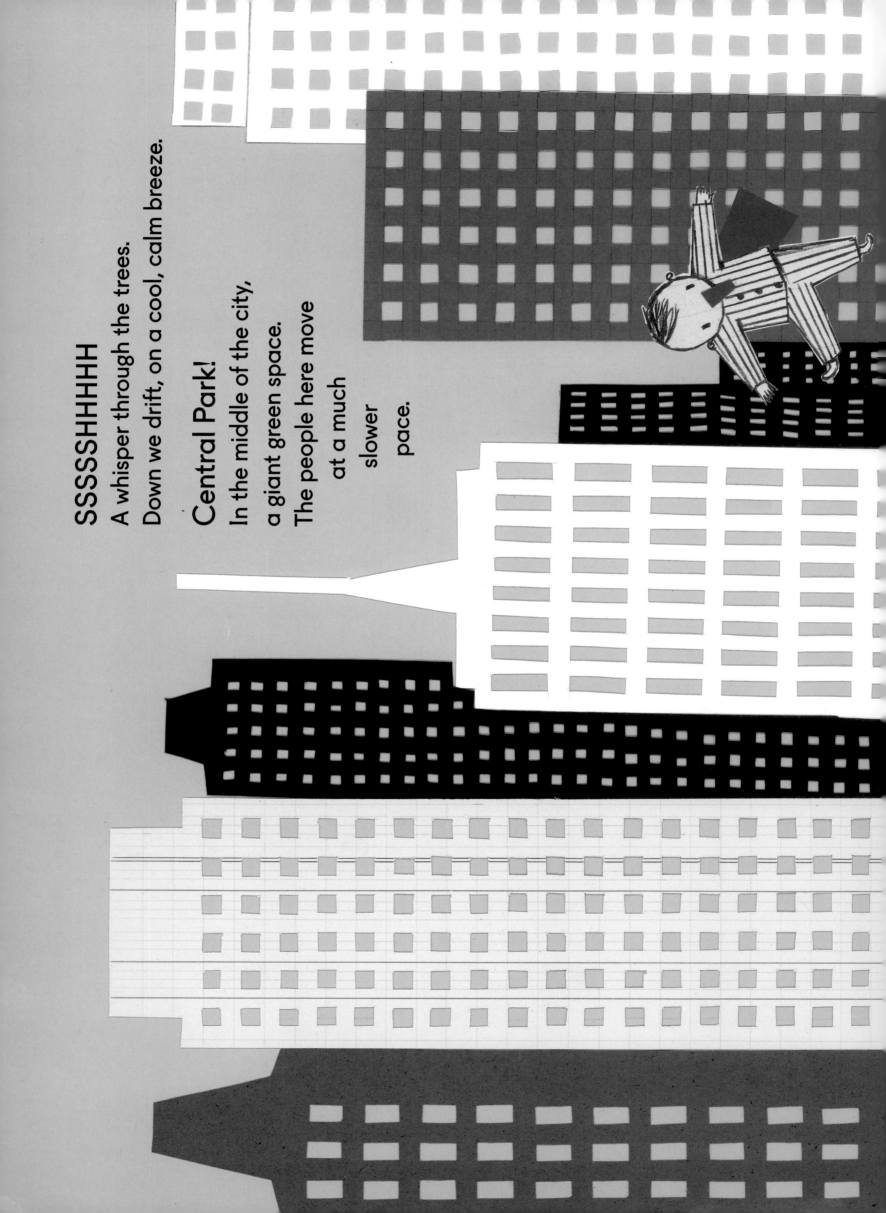

SSSSSHHHHH
A whisper through the trees.
Down we drift, on a cool, calm breeze.

Central Park!
In the middle of the city,
a giant green space.
The people here move
at a much
slower
pace.

SHOWS

BROADWAY

PALACE

YES

Stars

I've never seen a street this bright,
So many stars and names in lights!

Crowds flock to see the show.
The queue is moving. Off we go!

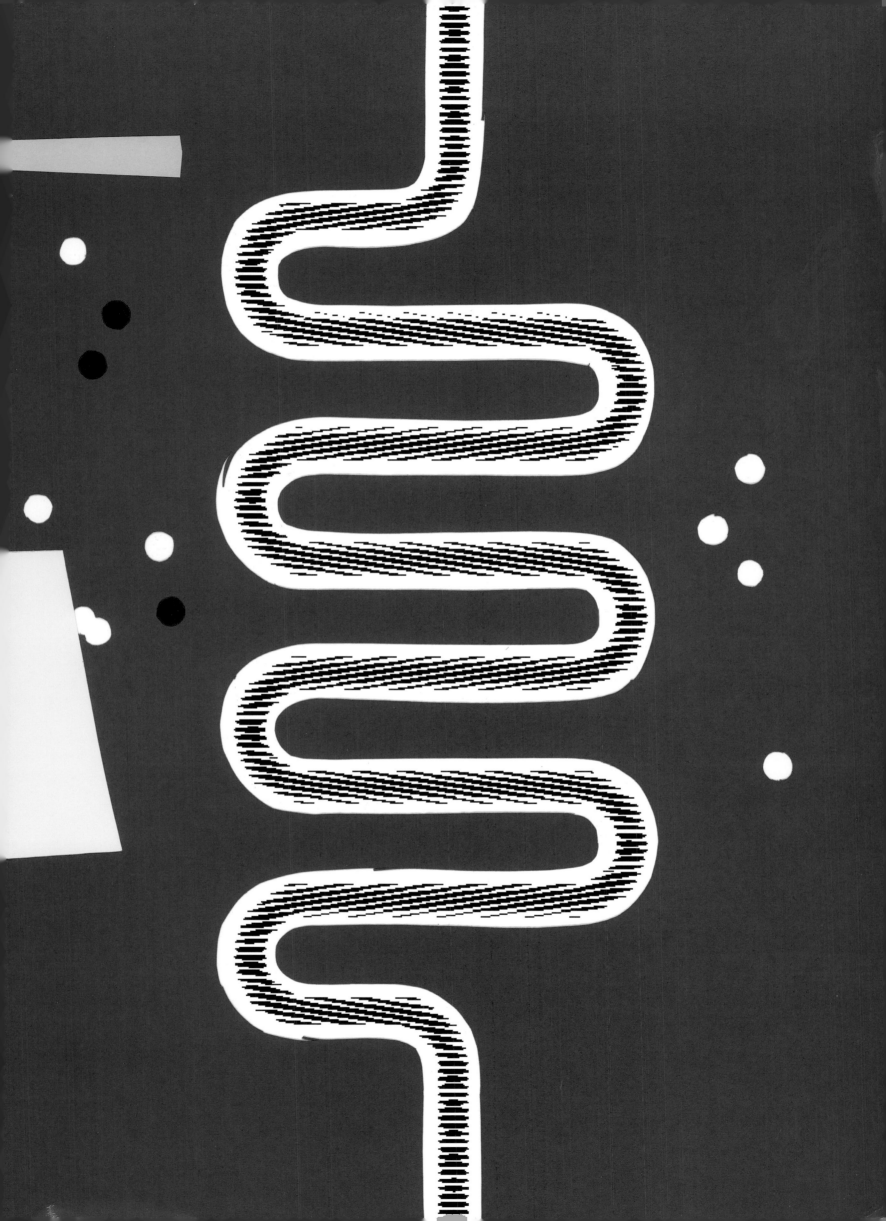

But far and above, the most beautiful sight,
Is this sparkling, dazzling city by night.

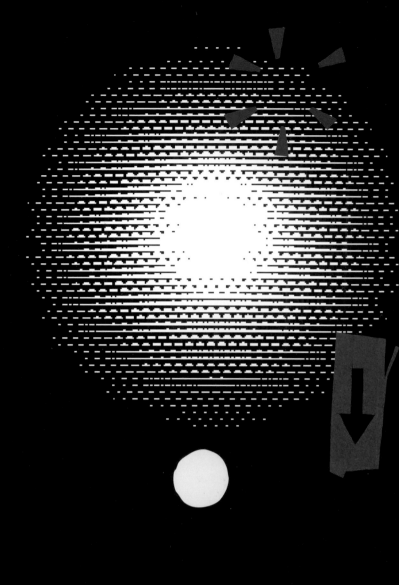

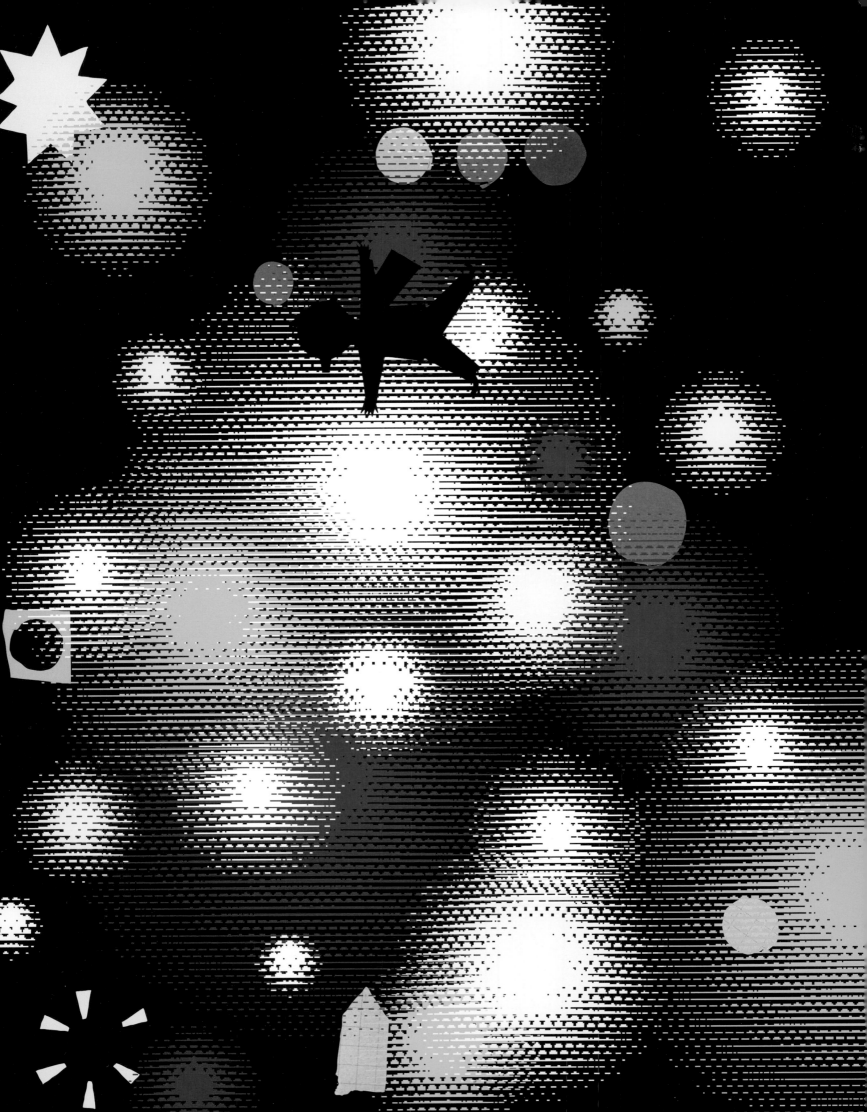

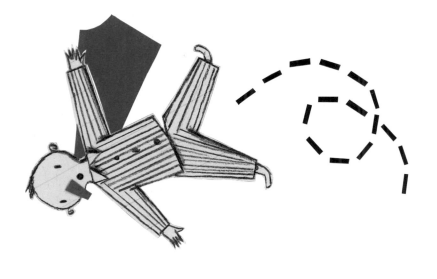

WHOA!
So high in the sky, it's no less busy;
This skyscraper forest is making me dizzy!

I need to stop and rest my head.
Striped pyjamas, back to bed!

Away in the distance, a voice is calling.
This means one thing…

...it's nearly morning.

Wakey, wakey, rise and shine!

Goodbye my friend,
Until next time.

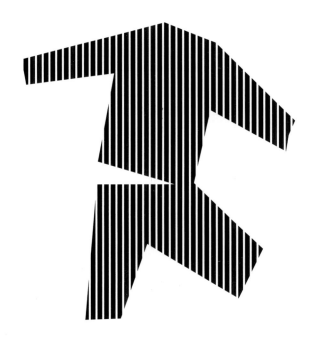

For Saiko, Tamao and Léo
ML

For Émilie and Violette
FB

PYJAMARAMA
Created by Frédérique Bertrand and Michaël Leblond,
with help from Frédéric Rey.

New York in Pyjamarama

ISBN: 978-1-907912-12-2

First published in French in 2011 under the title *New York en Pyjamarama*
by Editions du Rouergue, Arles, France.

This edition published in the UK by Phoenix Yard Books Ltd, 2012.

Phoenix Yard Books
Phoenix Yard
65 King's Cross Road
London
WC1X 9LW
www.phoenixyardbooks.com

1 3 5 7 9 10 8 6 4 2

A CIP catalogue record for this book is available from the British Library

Printed in China